Published in 2002 in the United States by Ragged Bears
413 Sixth Avenue
Brooklyn, New York 11215
www.raggedbears.com

Simultaneously published in the United Kingdom by Ragged Bears
Milborne Wick, Sherborne, Dorset DT9 4PW

CIP Data is available

First Edition
Printed and bound in China
ISBN: 1-929927-44-4
2 4 6 8 10 9 7 5 3 1

BOUNCING BABIES

MIKE BROWNLOW

RAGGED BEARS

BROOKLYN, NEW YORK • MILBORNE WICK, DORSET

Baby Sophie gives a yawn
When she wakes just after dawn.

Baby Benny on the mat
Sucks his toes - can you do that?

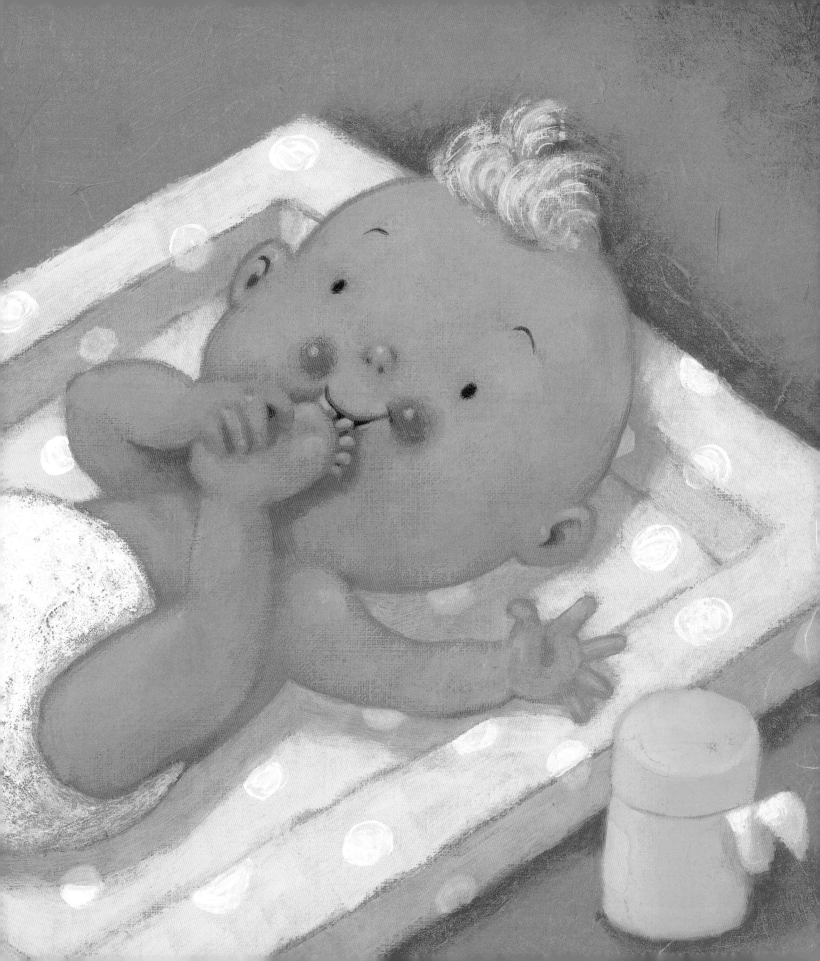

Anna pulls her sweater on
and disappears!
Now where's she gone?

Little baby Katherine
Dribbles milk all down her chin.

Bouncing baby Anthony
Sucks his thumb contentedly.

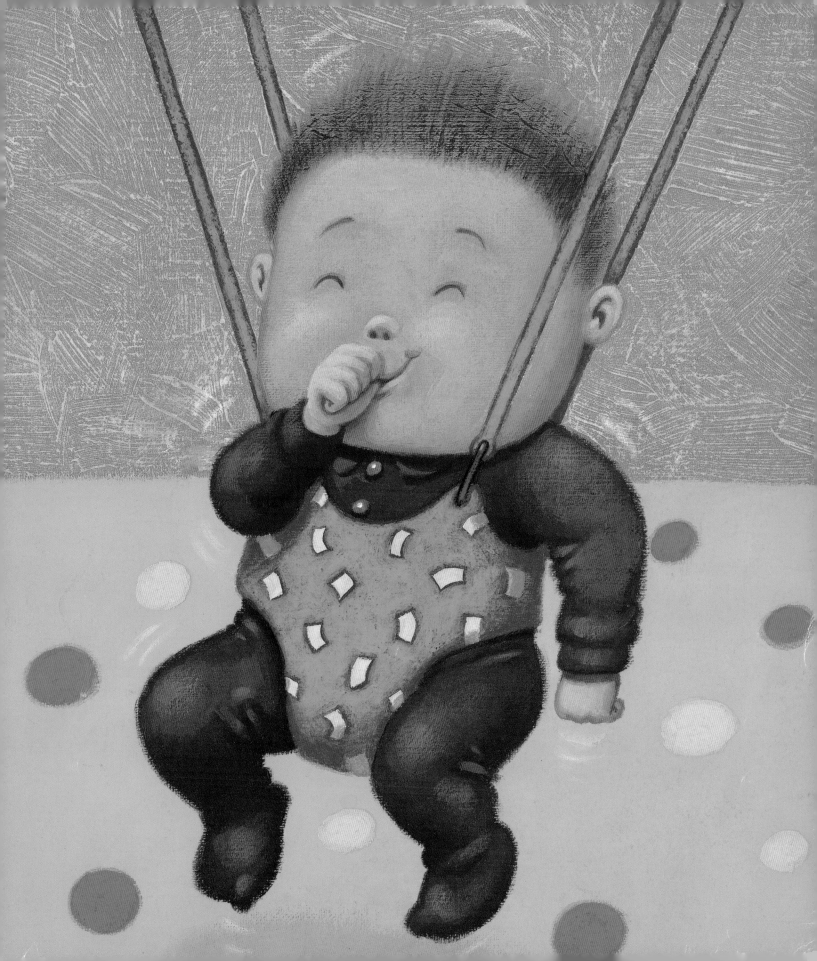

Little baby Ruby Rose
Always has a runny nose.

Tired little baby Freddy
Has a nap and so does Teddy.

Baby Daisy feels so pleased –
She's learned to crawl on
hands and knees!

Baby Jack with curly hair
Throws his supper everywhere!

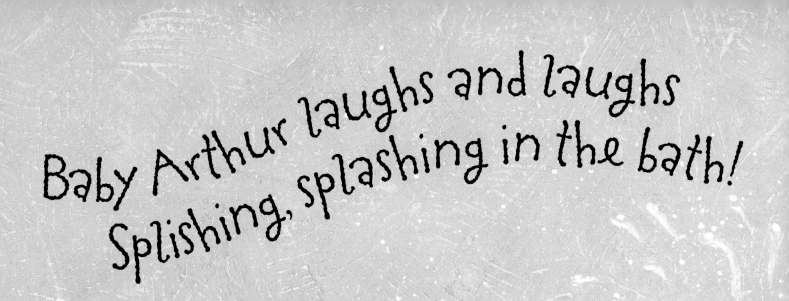

Baby Arthur laughs and laughs
Splishing, splashing in the bath!

Little babies made in heaven
Go to sleep at half-past seven.

But when the owl says twit-too-woo...

...Babies wake at half-past two!

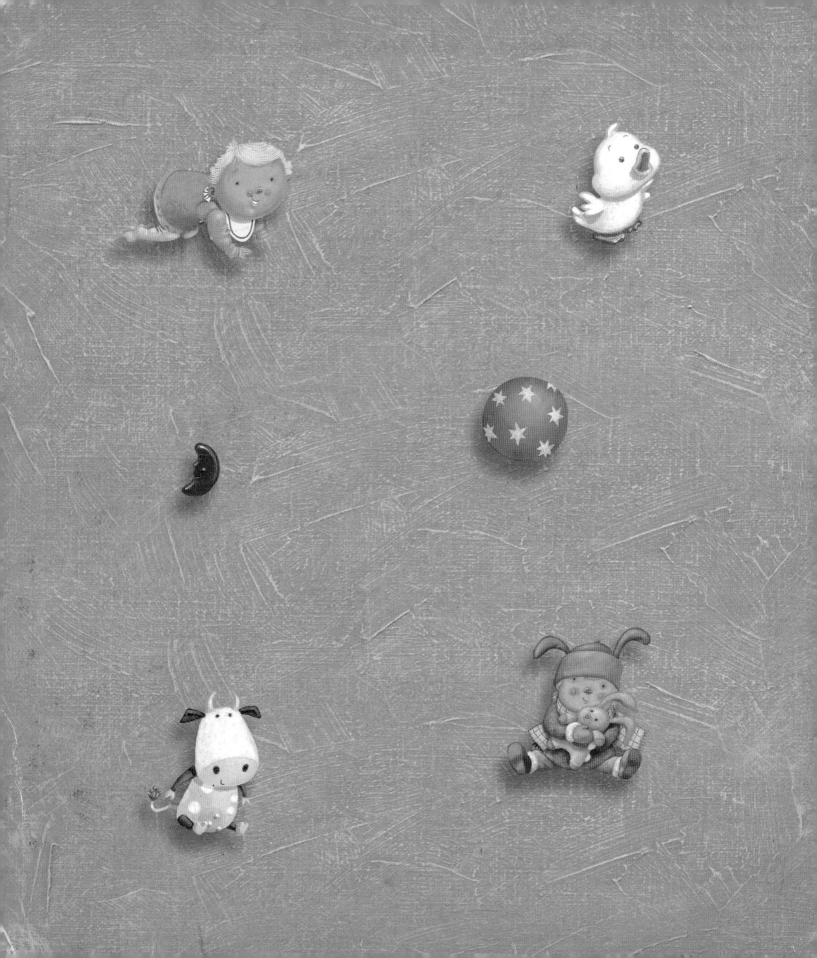